Henry Youle Hind

Report on the Waverley Gold District

with geological maps and sections

Henry Youle Hind

Report on the Waverley Gold District
with geological maps and sections

ISBN/EAN: 9783337255534

Printed in Europe, USA, Canada, Australia, Japan

Cover: Foto ©Andreas Hilbeck / pixelio.de

More available books at **www.hansebooks.com**

REPORT

ON THE

WAVERLEY GOLD DISTRICT,

WITH

GEOLOGICAL MAPS AND SECTIONS.

BY

HENRY YOULE HIND, M.A., F.R.G.S.

(Formerly of Trinity College, Toronto.)

MADE UNDER INSTRUCTIONS FROM THE HON. R. ROBERTSON, M.E.C.,
COMMISSIONER OF PUBLIC WORKS AND MINES.

HALIFAX, N. S.,
PRINTED BY CHARLES ANNAND,
1869.

Hon. Robert Robertson, M. E. C.,
Commissioner of Public Works and Mines.

Sir,—

I have the honor to submit to you my report on the Waverley Gold District, with accompanying Geological Maps and Sections, made in accordance with your instructions under date October 14th, 1868.

I have the honor to be,
Your obedient servant,
HENRY YOULE HIND.

Windsor, January, 1869.

MAPS AND SECTIONS ACCOMPANYING THIS REPORT.

1. Geological Map of Waverley Gold District, on a scale of 200 feet to the inch, shewing out-crop of the leads.

2. Reduced Map of No. 1 on a scale of 600 feet to the inch.

3. Vertical section of the District, from East to West, showing dislocations, &c., &c., on a scale of 200 feet to the inch.

4. General Section, showing structure of the country, on a scale of 1600 feet to the inch.

5. Vertical cross section through East Waverley, on a scale of 100 feet to the inch.

6. Nos. 1 to 5, Cross Sections in West Waverley, on a scale of 400 feet to the inch.

CONTENTS.

    I. Geographical Features.

   II. Geological Features.

  III. Dislocations.

  IV. Disposition of the out-crop of the strata.

   V. Characteristic rocks of the District.

  VI. Probable identification of gold-bearing groups of leads in different Districts.

 VII. Section on Range V., West Waverley, showing the different groups of leads, with some of the characteristic rocks with which each group is associated.

VIII. General structure of the leads.

  IX. Waverley leads.

   X. The "Gold Streak."

  XI. Gold at different depths.

 XII. Comparison between the Geological structure of Waverley and Mount Uniacke.

XIII. Comparison between Waverley and Lawrencetown.

XIV. Mining economies at Waverley—Mill work.

 XV. System of Mining.

XVI. General observations.

XVII. Age of the Gold-bearing Rocks of Nova Scotia.

REPORT.

I.—GEOGRAPHICAL FEATURES.

WAVERLEY Gold District is fourteen miles from Halifax, eleven of which are by rail to Rocky Lake station, and three from the station to the village situated in the centre of the district. The western boundary of the areas shown on the plan, is, however, not more than a mile and a quarter from Windsor Junction station, thirteen miles from Halifax.

Two well marked chains of lakes traverse the district from north to south. These lakes lie on the course of two nearly parallel dislocations or lines of disturbance, about 5,000 feet apart, and offer a fine illustration of the dependence of geographical outline on geological structure. The westerly chain embraces Third Lake, Three Mile Lake and Fishing Lake, with their connecting streams, in the aggregate two miles and a half long. Their waters flow from north to south to the vicinity of Fishing Lake, they then strike across the country to Lake William, which, with a large sheet of water named Lake Thomas, belongs to the eastern chain, whose waters flow from south to north, and ultimately reach the Bay of Fundy by the Shubenacadie River. The eastern shores of Lakes Thomas and William are bold and abrupt, having a mean altitude of 200 feet above their surface, and when viewed in connection with the low country occupied by the lakes named, at once suggest to the observer a disturbance of considerable magnitude in geological structure. The district is divided into two portions, called East and West Waverley. East Waverley lies to the east of Lakes William and Thomas ; West Waverley to the west of those lakes.

No surface within the limits of the district is elevated more than 330 feet above Lake William, or about 380 feet above the sea. The highest point is on the north boundary of East Waverley. The summit in West Waverley is on the outcrop of the Union or Taylor lead, and is 116 feet above Lake William.

On a line of section running nearly due east and west, along the axis of the Anticlinal in West Waverley, the highest point is 98 feet, while east of Lake Thomas on the continuation of the same section, the land rises abruptly to 200 feet above the lake.

Subjoined are a number of longitudinal and transverse sections, which may be found useful.

SECTION FROM LAKE THOMAS TO WEST MAIN DISLOCATION—AREAS 181 TO 211—WEST WAVERLEY.

	Distance.		Altitude.	
South line of Range VIII., Level of Lake Thomas	0 feet	......	0	feet.
	100 "	......	30.95 "	
	250 "	......	47.90 "	
	400 "	......	49.30 "	
	550 "	......	41.90 "	
	700 "	......	38.85 "	
	850 "	......	43.05 "	
	1000 "	......	55.30 "	
American Hill	1150 "	......	86.10 "	
On axis of anticlinal, North line of Range VIII.......	1200 "	......	69.60 "	
	1250 "	......	50.50 "	
	1300 "	......	32.15 "	
Muddy Pond	1450 "	......	2.50 "	
	1670 "	......	16.85 "	
	1720 "	......	34.20 "	
	1750 "	......	40.00 "	
	1840 "	......	38.00 "	
	1900 "	.....	36.45 "	
	2050 "	......	42.60 "	
	2200 "	......	58.65 "	
	2350 "	......	53.45 "	
	2500 "	......	57.80 "	
	2610 "	......	76.30 "	
	2650 "	......	82.20 "	
	2680 "	......	93.35 "	
	2800 "	......	94.65 "	
DeWolfe's Engine Shaft.......2950 "		......	98.35 "	

	Distance.		Altitude.
	3100 feet	......	96.50 feet.
	3250 "	......	89.45 "
	3400 "	......	78.60 "
	3550 "	......	68.25 "
	3700 "	......	62.00 "
	3850 "	......	52.25 "
	4000 "	......	41.25 "
	4150 "	......	34.55 "
	4300 "	......	33.00 "
	4450 "	......	43.30 "
Burkner's Crusher	4600 "	......	30.25 "
	4690 "	......	48.70 "
	4750 "	.....	53.60 "
	4900 "	......	48.90 "
	5050 "	......	45.70 "
West Dislocation............	5200 "	......	53.70 "

SOUTH LINE OF RANGE VIII.—EAST WAVERLEY.

	Distance.		Altitude.
Lake Thomas................	0 feet	......	0 feet.
Barrel Quartz	850 "	......	131.40 "
	1000 "	......	169.60 "
	1150 "	......	184.35 "
	1300 "	......	180.80 "
	1450 "	......	195.15 "
	1600 "	......	187.55 "
	1750 "	......	191.45 "
	1900 "	......	200.15 "

CROSS SECTIONS FROM NORTH TO SOUTH—EAST WAVERLEY.

Commencing 150 feet south of the north line of Range II., on line between areas 170 and 171.

	Distance.		Altitude above Lake Thomas.
1st station	0 feet	......	238.85 feet
	150 "	......	238.05 "
	400 "	......	236.55 "
	650 "	......	221.30 "
	900 "	......	204.95 "
	1150 "	......	200.90 "

	Distance.	Altitude above Lake Thomas.
Brook from Willis' Lake	1400 feet	192.20 feet.
Cross east and west line of section.	1650 "	200.15 "
Anticlinal axis	1900 "	219.10 "
	2150 "	229.35 "
	2400 "	249.60 "
	2650 "	252.90 "
	2900 "	258.75 "
	3150 "	266.55 "

Commencing on north line of Range II., on line between areas 177 and 178.

	Distance.	Altitude above Lake Thomas.
1st station	0 feet	293.30 feet.
	250 "	278.65 "
	500 "	263.40 "
	750 "	254.80 "
	1000 "	245.65 "
	1250 "	207.90 "
	1500 "	177.30 "
	1750 "	164.30 "
	2000 "	166.80 "
Brook from Willis' Lake	2250 "	131.40 "
	2500 "	131.50 "
	2750 "	148.75 "
	3000 "	199.30 "
	3080 "	188.75 "
	3110 "	204.65 "
	3163 "	222.95 "

CROSS SECTION FROM NORTH TO SOUTH—WEST WAVERLEY.

Commencing on north boundary of District, on line between areas 221 and 222.

	Distance.	Altitude above Lake Thomas.
North line of District	0 feet	95.65 feet.
	200 "	66.80 "
	250 "	44.30 "
	450 "	41.90 "

	Distance.		Altitude.
	670 feet	......	58.65 feet.
	700 "	......	68.60 "
	950 "	......	83.15 "
	1200 "	......	91.45 "
Burkner's pumping shaft......	1450 "	......	84.30 "
Axis of anticlinal	1700 "	......	78.60 "
	1950 "	......	77.30 "
	2200 "	......	83.90 "
	2450 "	......	79.55 "
	2499 "	......	67.27 "
	2570 "	......	52.25 "
	2700 "	......	55.80 "
	2890 "	......	60.75 "
	2950 "	......	51.60 "

II. GEOLOGICAL FEATURES.

In West Waverley there are few rock exposures; coarse drift varying from three feet to fifty in depth, and in great part composed of gravels and clays, enclosing unworn masses of local origin, covers the surface. A few boulders of granite, derived from a range some miles to the north, are scattered here and there. In East Waverley, rock exposures are numerous, and in general the drift is shallow; it contains comparatively few detrital masses until the summit plateau is attained near and beyond Lake Willis.

The strata at Waverley are arranged in the form of an elongated elliptical dome, whose longest axis is from East to West, or more correctly on a course N. 85 ° E.

The first movement which led to the present attitude of the strata was from South to North, by which the beds were thrown into a huge anticlinal fold or undulation, one of many parallel and similar undulations which traverse the country.

A very feeble conception can now be formed by superficial observation of the original enormous magnitude of these huge waves of rock which ridged the surface of the Province. Whether denudation took place as fast as the uplift, or whether the undulations attained their maximum altitude, partially or wholly undenuded, it is certain that not less than 9000 feet, in vertical thickness, belonging to one rock series, have been removed from the present surface of Waverley Gold District.

The direction of the crest or axis of this undulation is from the east to west, and the force which occasioned it, operated sufficiently long to throw it over towards the north, hence on the south side of the anticlinal the dips are much less than on the north side, and at the depth of four or five hundred feet, the strata on the north side of the anticlinal will have an overturn dip, and a vertical section from north to south would show the beds to have been thrust over in the form of a pot-hook or letter S.

Long subsequently to the operation of the force which occasioned the east and west anticlinal, another movement from west to east produced a low north and south anticlinal, whose axis appears to lie near Lake Willis. It is this movement which has been the cause of the enormous breaks or dislocations already alluded to, as affecting the geographical outline of the country. The result of these anticlinals, crossing one another nearly at right angles, is seen in the long elliptical dome-shaped form, tilted over to the north, which the strata at Waverley now exhibit.

III.—DISLOCATIONS.

If no break or fracture had taken place in the strata, when the low north and south anticlinal was in process of folding, West Waverley, as part of a Gold District, would remain unrecognized. At the east dislocation or line of fracture, an upthrow to the extent of 570 feet took place, and five thousand one hundred feet west of this the upthrow at the west dislocation was upwards of 750 feet. Nor were these the only movements which resulted from the fracture, the entire country between the great dislocations, comprising nearly the whole of West Waverley, was moved as it were on a pivot or centre of motion; the thrust being to the north on the Lake

Thomas side for about 520 feet, and on the west or Fishing Lake side, 180 feet to the south. The pivot or centre of the twist lay between areas 200 and 221.

Simultaneously with this oscillatory motion, the strata were squeezed from west to east in the form of an arch, causing an upthrow of the crown of the arch about areas 222 and 223 to the extent of fifteen hundred feet, and bringing the walls of the dislocations three hundred and seventy feet nearer to one another; that is to say: if no squeeze from west to east had taken place, the walls of the break would have been 370 feet further distant from one another than they now are.

The several movements which have led to the present structure of West Waverley may be recapitulated as follows :—

1st. The great East and West overturn anticlinal.
2nd. The low North and South Cross anticlinal, which produced a fracture in the strata 5100 feet from one wall to another, as well as—
3rd. An upthrow of 570 feet on the east side, with a shove to the north of 520 feet, and on the west side an upthrow of 780 feet, and a shove to the south of 180 feet.
4th. A squeeze of the strata between the walls of the break to the extent of 370 feet, by lateral pressure, probably from west to east, and causing—
5th. An upthrow of the crown of the arch, resulting from the lateral pressure, to the extent of fifteen hundred feet.

The west dislocation is sharp and well defined, the line of fracture dipping easterly at an angle of about 60 degrees. The east dislocation is distinguished by a broad belt of disturbed strata, the rock having a brecciated structure. The Barrel Quartz of Laidlaw Hill, if it had maintained its dip undisturbed to a point 600 feet west of the centre of the bridge, ought to be about 500 feet below the surface on the axis of the anticlinal, and dipping westerly at an angle of 25 degrees; it is, nevertheless, found at the surface in a vertical position, or nearly so, with a strike S. 79 E. Throughout this broken belt, which may be 200 feet broad, the rock is much disturbed, the irregularity being caused by the grinding effect of the combined upthrow and shove to the north.

It may be described as a " Breccia " or rock composed of angular fragments cemented together.

In other Gold Districts dislocations exist of great magnitude. At Sherbrooke there is an enormous dislocation running up St. Mary's River, but no accurate details are known respecting it. Its course is from north to south. At Montague, there is a dislocation also running nearly due north and south through areas 1247, 1153, 1047, &c. This has been accompanied by a shove to the north of 43 feet. At Lawrencetown there appears to have been a dislocation of considerable magnitude, which has thrown the leads on the east side about 10 degrees out of their original course. At Renfrew there is a considerable twist in the leads on the Free Claim, occasioned by a crush or squeeze from west to east, throwing the leads from 30 to 50 feet out of their course, and producing fissures in the strata which were subsequently filled with auriferous quartz and carbonate of lime, forming short segregated veins. All of these great movements may have been contemporaneous, and all connected with the system of cross or north and south anticlinals, which has so remarkably affected the Waverley District.

In East Waverley, minor faults, probably upthrows, are numerous. The fracture dips to the east at an angle of 60 degrees, and they preserve nearly the same course as the great dislocations. Small shoves to the north are also visible, and just beyond the limits of the District there is a good illustration exposed in the bare rock forming the summit of the highest escarpment, and about one hundred yards to the east. Here, between belts of quartzite, having a course N. 85 E., is a broad band of slate, twisted so as to have a strike N. 45 E.

IV.—DISPOSITION OF THE OUTCROP OF THE STRATA.

All the so-called worked " veins " at Waverley have a bedded structure, and are interstratified with the slates and quartzites; consequently the outcrop of the strata, which must necessarily be symmetrical with that of the interstratified " veins," is of the first importance in endeavoring to obtain a knowledge of the structural geology of the District.

With the exception of the small faults, to which allusion has been made, the strata in East Waverley are perfectly symmetrical, and the outcrops of the quartzites, the bands of slate and the leads, assume the form of concentric halves of ellipses as shown on the plan. This disposition of the outcrop is due to the angle of denudation being less than the angle of dip. It may be readily illustrated by means of a number of thick sheets of paper bent in an arched form, slightly flattened at the summit to represent the east and west anticlinal, then tilted westerly at an angle of 25 degrees to represent the north and south anticlinal. The upper portion being now cut clean off horizontally, the exposed edges of the leaves will represent the outcrop of the strata, and have the form of concentric semi-ellipses.

Between the west dislocation and the railway the rocks are also symmetrically arranged, and a number of observations taken in the railway cuttings showed that the axis of the east and west anticlinal at East Waverley, if prolonged, would meet and coincide with the axis of the anticlinal where it is crossed by the railway.

In West Waverley, between the dislocations, the axis is twisted as represented on the plan, and the outcrop of the strata and leads is that of a series of concentric semi-ellipses, much flattened or compressed at the sides, and with a northerly bend at its western extremity.

V. CHARACTERISTIC ROCKS OF THE DISTRICT.

The lowest or oldest rock seen within the present limits of the district is a thin bed of Argillite, or Clay Slate, dark greenish-gray in colour, but weathering reddish-brown in patches. This rock occurs 24 feet below the Barrel Quartz. The highest, or newest rock, is found on the east side of the West Main dislocation, and is 1500 feet vertically above the thin band of Argillite.

The known gold-bearing beds of quartz lie in a belt eleven hundred feet thick above the Argillite. But these numbers are far from representing the actual thickness of the auriferous strata. Several gold-bearing leads have been found within a distance of 4600 feet from the axis of the anticlinal, showing a known thickness of auriferous rocks exceeding three thousand five hundred feet. At Renfrew the thickness of the known and worked gold-bearing belt is about five thousand feet; and at Mount Uniacke it is certainly not much less. At Lawrencetown the thickness of the known belt is about 1800 feet; but the country to the south and north of the worked or discovered leads is still unexplored in this district. The anticlinal here involves a shallow synclinal near its summit. The entire thickness of the auriferous strata in Nova Scotia is stated by Mr. Campbell to be far in excess of the dimensions given above. (1.)

From what is known of the distribution of gold in the leads in different districts, it appears probable that the richest auriferous zone lies near the base of the series, and thus affords encouragement to the expectation that districts will be discovered where the base is brought to the surface, and that far richer deposits of the precious metal will eventually be worked than have hitherto been met with. (2.)

It appears to be a common feature in most of the districts that some of the richest mines are located near the crown of the Anticlinal; consequently in the lowest accessible strata. Hence, other things being equal, it is always advisable to sink a main shaft near the axis, because lower beds in the series may be thus reached than by placing the main shaft in any other position.

In the Waverley series, eleven hundred feet thick, are comprised massive beds of "Whin" and quartzite, interstratified with thin beds of clay slate, which sometimes assumes a micaceous form. Under the general name "Whin" are included

---

1. Mr. Selwyn estimates the auriferous strata in Victoira (Australia) to be not less than 35,000 feet thick.

2. This generalization will be better understood when it is known, as stated subsequently in the text, that probably many hundred feet of strata are exposed, and the leads in them worked, at Mount Uniacke, which lie *underneath* the Barrel Quartz at Waverley. If it should be proved that the richest beds lie at the base of the series, cross sections on the course of the great anticlinals may lead to the discovery of the upturned and denuded edges of these lower beds, where in all probability leads of unusual richness and equality in the distribution of the precious metal may be discovered.

a variety of rocks which are correctly known as Diorites, Diabase, Dolerite, &c.; but for the sake of simplicity these will all be comprehended in the general description under the term "Whin"; the different strata in Nova Scotia Mining Districts being divided popularly into "Slate" and "Whin."

Very considerable differences exist between the several beds of "Whin," Quartztic and Slate, and as it appears to be a characteristic feature of some gold fields in Nova Scotia (Waverley, Lawrencetown, Mount Uniacke,) that certain groups of gold-bearing leads are associated with particular varieties of Whin, Quartzite or Slate, it becomes a study of considerable importance, not only to distinguish carefully between the different beds, but also to group them accurately according to their position. The possible results of this discrimination may be estimated by the following considerations :—

VI.—PROBABLE IDENTIFICATION OF GOLD-BEARING GROUPS OF LEADS IN DIFFERENT DISTRICTS.

There is strong evidence to prove that the Gold-bearing rocks of Lawrencetown, Waverley, Mount Uniacke, as well as other districts, are not only of the same geological age, but of the same geological horizon, and that the so-called " veins," " leads " or " lodes," in which the gold is chiefly found, are true beds of quartz of aqueous origin, and formed by deposition in the same manner as the associated quartzites and slates, with which they are interstratified, and indefinitely prolonged in all directions.[1] For instance : a lustrous, curly plumbaginous slate, is found at Waverley associated with rich gold-bearing beds of quartz. A similar slate, so closely resembling the Waverley rock, that hand specimens cannot be distinguished one from the other, is found at Lawrencetown, also associated with gold-bearing leads, and with " Whin " like that at Waverley. In a less marked degree, a plumbaginous slate is found at Mount Uniacke, preserving a certain vertical distance from a very characteristic coarse quartzite. This coarse quartzite is also found at Waverley in

---

1. See an article on this subject by the writer of this Report in the April Supplement to the Mining Gazette, Halifax, 1868.

the same relation to the plumbaginous slate as at Mount Uniacke. The probable inference from these facts is that the groups of gold-bearing veins worked at Waverley and Lawrencetown in connection with the plumbaginous slate are identical, and may be found at Mount Uniacke ; also, that any group of leads found at Waverley at an ascertained distance from the plumbaginous slate or coarse quartzite may be searched for with success at Lawrencetown or Mount Uniacke, and *vice versa.*

Hence the information acquired in one district becomes available in another district, provided it is judiciously applied, with due precautions as to variations in the thickness of the slaty and quartzose beds. In one part of Mount Uniacke the bed of coarse quartzite was found to be 380 feet thick, in which no parting of slate was seen where the section was made, but the gradations from coarse to fine quartzite were very distinct. At Waverley the supposed same bed of quartzite has one known lead and two partings of slate, which were seen on one side of the anticlinal. On the other side several thin partings were recognized. These sections are given in detail under the head " Barrel Quartz Lead," where the information they convey is discussed.

Another reason why special attention should be given to the mineral characters and order of occurrence of different strata is to be found in their disposition in the form of anticlinal or synclinal folds. The auriferous quartz lodes on the north side of an anticlinal will be found in corresponding positions on the south side, proper allowance being made for difference in dip. The form of the anticlinal at Waverley being that of a slight overturn to the north, the quartz beds on the south side will be further from the axis than their continuation on the north side, the difference being dependant on the dip, or the tilt to the north. At Mount Uniacke, where the overturn is to the south, the reverse of this will be the case.

To enumerate and describe all the different beds at Waverley, would be at present impossible, as no complete section is visible, but sufficient can be seen in different exposures and shafts to permit an approximate grouping of the leads, for the sake of convenience, and a brief description of the characteristic strata with which each provisional group is asso-ciated.

In using the conventional term " lead," the so-called "veins," "lodes" or "leads," are regarded as thin beds of quartz of aqueous origin, and for the most part deposited under similar conditions as the strata with which they are interstratified. This interesting and important subject will be discussed at length in subsequent pages.

VII.—SECTION ON RANGE V., WEST WAVERLEY, SHOWING THE DIFFERENT GROUPS OF LEADS, WITH SOME OF THE CHARACTERISTIC ROCKS WITH WHICH EACH GROUP IS ASSOCIATED.

Rocks in ascending order—Thickness of section 1290 feet.

I.—BARREL QUARTZ GROUP.

1. Whin—thickness unknown.
2. Slate approaching argillite, greenish grey internally, weathering ferruginous brown, with purple patches.
    I. Lead 4 inches.
3. Whin.
4. Argillite—greenish gray.
    II. Barrel Quartz Lead, 6 inches to 16 inches.
5. Whin, passing into fine micaceous slate, interstratified with bands of slate.
6. III. Slate Lead.
7. IV. Lead.
8. V. Slate Lead.

Total thickness 120 feet. Dip horizontal, or at very low angle. This group forms the flat crown of the anticlinal. (1).

II.—ROSE GROUP.

1. Whin interstratified with thin bands of slate.
    I. DeWolfe Lead.
2. Greenish gray banded slates. The bands or stripes ½ a line to 2 lines broad, and enclose brilliant crystals of arsenical iron pyrites.

(1.) The names given to the different leads are those by which they are generally known in the district. As certain leads have the same name, or are differently named by different miners, their identification can only be established by reference to the plan.

3. Dark bluish gray slate, loaded with crystals of iron pyrites. In some layers the crystals are very minute, and weathering brown, give to the mass a speckled appearance. Interstratified with No. 2.

II. "Large Lead" holding "nuggetty gold."

III. Rose Lead, 4 to 6 inches. On area 193 dips N. W. angle 60 ; on area 256 dips S. angle 21 deg.

4. A fine-grained Whin, holding a few pebbles of the dark bluish-gray slate.

5. Dark bluish-gray slate.

Thickness 60 feet.

III.—TAYLOR GROUP.

I. Concretionary Quartzite upwards of 70 feet thick. The concretions are very marked in the exposures of this rock in East Waverley. They frequently resemble fossil forms, and it is subsequently shown that this quartzite is fossiliferous.

Number of Veins.	Thickness.	Remarks.
1	4 inches	
2	1½ "	
3	1 "	
4	4 "	
5	16 "	No. VI. Lead on Plan.
6	4 "	
7	2 "	
8	6 "	
9	2 "	
10	9 "	
11	4 "	
12	9 "	
13	I "	
14	14 "	
15	2 "	
16	4 "	
17	18 "	
18	3 "	
19	2 "	
20	1 "	
21	5 "	South Taylor.
22	16 "	

Number of Veins.		Thickness.	Remarks.
23	....	2 inches.	
24	....	10 "	North Taylor.
25	....	.3 "	
26	....	3 "	
27	....	4 "	

Breadth of this section, 160 feet. Total thickness, 320 feet.

The Taylor Group is distinguished by the occurrence of thin bands of plumbaginous slate, interstratified with gray Whin and ferruginous slate. The plumbaginous slate is sometimes curly, and of a brilliant metallic lustre; streak ash gray: splits into numerous fine layers, with smooth brilliant black surfaces.

It occurs 120 feet south of No. 12 lead; also at leads Nos. 10 and 11. At and near lead No. 6 is a banded slate with plumbaginous surfaces or partings. The dark blue portion is compact, hard, and holds minute crystals of arsenical iron. The lighter coloured stripes or bands contain much silica, and are from half a line to two lines in breadth.

IV.—TUDOR GROUP.

1. Heavy-bedded gray Whin, containing large crystals and nodules of arsenical iron pyrites.

        I. The Tudor Lead.

        II. The North Lead.

2. Heavy-bedded gray Whin, holding pebbles of blue-black slate, and thin bands of blue-black slate.

        III. Twin Leads.

Thickness, 190 feet.

V.—SOUTH LEAD GROUP.

1. Thin banded slates, with dark-gray slates loaded with small crystals of arsenical iron pyrites. Massive beds of Whin with small crystals and scales of arsenical iron pyrites, interstratified with blue-black slate. The blue-black slate is also seen in position on the north side of the anticlinal on the road.

        I. South Lead.

        II. Numerous leads lying south of the South Lead.

Thickness, 600 feet.

RECAPITULATION.

I.   Barrel Quartz Group, with 5 known leads, 120 feet.
II. Rose Group,   " 3   "   "   60   "
III. Taylor   ....   " 27 "   "   320   "
IV. Tudor   ....   " 4   "   "   190   "
V.   South Group .....   " 7   "   "   600   "
                                              ____
                                              1290   "

VIII.—GENERAL STRUCTURE OF THE LEADS.

When leads are worked in Whin, they are almost always found to be bounded by distinct walls; when Whin is on one side and slate on the other, the wall on the Whin side is generally well defined, while on the slate side it is not only irregular, but the slate is frequently seen interstratified with the lead.

The popular impression that all quartz is of igneous origin, and was injected from "below," is common among miners in Nova Scotia, and much loss of capital has resulted from this mistaken notion. No evidence has yet been met with in any district to my knowledge which give the faintest color to this view as far as the leads in Nova Scotia are concerned.

It is often urged that the well-defined Whin wall is a proof that the lead is not a stratified bed of quartz of contemporaneous age, but an injected or segregated vein, either filling a fracture or replacing other strata which have been removed in a state of solution. It may, however, be remarked that the line of demarkation between slate and Whin often exhibits a true wall, and that if quartz be substituted for a thin band of slate, an exact reproduction of a lead in all its details is effected. Hence, what is true of quartz, as far as the wall is concerned, must be true of the slate under similar conditions, but no one suggests the subsequent introduction of thin bands of slate, much less their injection. The wall in both instances often gives proofs of movement.

Among the most remarkable peculiarities of the leads are the markings on the quartz and on the enclosing rock, whether Whin or hard compact slate. These markings vary from slickensides to huge rolls, several feet apart, and sometimes a foot in the swell. They are found in the slates, remote from leads, and often resemble ripple marks. To Mr. Campbell the credit is due of first calling particular attention to these markings, and Dr. Hunt, likewise impressed with their importance in regard to the structural geology of the Gold Districts, says:

" Mr. Campbell has called special attention to what he has called the grain or reed-like marking often impressed on the surface of the beds in a direction parallel to the east and west axes of folding, and he points out that the angle of dip, eastward or westward, of these markings on the crown of the great anticlinals enables us to detect the transverse or north and south lines of undulation, which have at a subsequent period disturbed the horizontality of the east and west anticlinal folds. The markings in question often appear as rib-like ridges or flutings, which are most conspicuous on the surface of the auriferous quartz layers and the enclosing beds. On the summit of the anticlinal folds they are sometimes so large, and so well defined, as to give to the layers a wrinkled or corrugated form, producing what is designated in the region as barrel quartz, and has by some observers been compared to the ripples on water, and by others to that parallel arrangement of logs which is seen on what is called a corduroy road. The best known samples of this is at Waverley, but it is also seen at Montague, Oldham, and at Upper Stewiacke."

A few yards west of the West main dislocation at Waverley, a fine illustration of these corrugations is visible in the slates. The resemblance to ripple marks at the first glance is very striking, but a closer examination shows that the corrugation is not on the same plane as the bedding, and consequently the force which produced it must have been other than water.

The direction of the axis of the small undulations is such, that they might well have been produced during the folding of the greater or east and west anticlinal, but the occurrence of similar corrugations in other districts, at angles nearly approaching forty-five degrees, where there is no evidence of a cross anticlinal of such magnitude, gives colour to the supposition that these markings were not necessarily associated with the first folding, and that they are untrustworthy guides in relation to that movement.

At Montague and at Mount Uniacke, there are small and

large undulations and markings, which do not appear to have had any connection with the east and west folding, but it is very probable that they were connected with local disturbances in those districts, and may form valuable assistants in discovering the displacements. Under all circumstances they are well worthy of study, and such distinguishing characteristics may eventually be found as will enable them to be separated, and referred to the force which produced them, whether occasioning a fold or a dislocation.

They have, however, an especial bearing on the structure of numerous leads, which give indisputable evidence of motion, either in their body or at one wall. The coincidence between the direction of the ripples on the slates at Waverley and the dip of the rocks resulting from the cross anticlinal, is so marked that in this instance they may with propriety be referred to the first folding; and the force which occasioned the ripples caused also a bodily sliding to a small extent of one bed of strata over another, and the production of a fissure which was subsequently filled with quartz and carbonate of lime constituting a segregated vein.— Sometimes the fracture and sliding took place in or near the middle of a bed of quartz. At Mount Uniacke, for instance, there is a four-foot lead, which has a fracture near the centre, partially filled (subsequently) with arsenical iron pyrites, and in the cavities the crystals of quartz are seen with their apices pointing towards each other. The same peculiarity is not unfrequently observed in large leads. At Waverley the movement has occurred between the quartz and the Whin, or between the quartz and hard slate, or in bands of slate, and in all cases slickensides, reed-like markings, ripples and small undulations have been produced. In the Barrel Quartz no sliding motion is distinguishable, for the corrugations extend far into the overlying Whin rock until they assume the form of a series of connected arches five, six and even seven feet in width. The corrugations are by no means confined to the quartz lead, but spread out, fan-like, into the overlying rock. At Montague the ripples or swells are at an angle of 45°, and are frequently from five to eight feet apart, and the swell rises as much as six inches above the plane of the bedding, the laminæ of the wall rock conforming to it.

At Lawrencetown there are similar large ripples, but at an angle of about 30 degrees. The leads in question, both at Montague and Lawrencetown, are synclinal forms. It is a popular belief that in the vicinity of these swells the lead is more productive than between them. It appears to be well established at Montague that the nodules of arsenical iron pyrites containing free gold, are more numerous and of larger proportions close to the swell than at a distance from it. But lenticular masses of arsenical iron pyrites are found in the Whin, remote from any visible vein, unconnected with one another, and sometimes lying at right angles to the bedding.

At Hammond Plains there are immense beds of feebly auriferous quartz, as much as 20 feet thick, and in these crys-tals of oxide of zinc are numerous, besides numerous cavities lined with crystals of calcareous spar ; the surfaces of the crys-tals are spangled with cubical iron pyrites. At Renfrew, where the strata have evidently slid over one another, crystals of calcareous spar are common, and sometimes form as much of the lead as the rich gold bearing quartz itself ; these occur on the Free Claim, where a considerable twisting of the strata has taken place, and short unconnected, but thick auriferous veins fill the cavities formed by the movement, which are newer than and wholly distinct from the bedded leads, con-temporaneous with the strata. While the gold which the bedded leads contain, in common with the other metals, was most probably derived from the oceanic waters from which the quartz was deposited, the gold in the short segregated veins of subsequent origin was transferred from the bedded leads or auriferous interstratified slates.

Dr. Hunt expresses his opinion somewhat decidedly respect-ing the origin of the quartz leads. He says,—" So far as my present observation goes, I think that to describe them other-wise than as interstratified beds, would be to give a false notion of their geognostic relations." (1).

(1.) GOLD REGION OF NOVA SCOTIA.

"The laminated structure of many of the lodes, and the intercalation between their layers of thin continuous films or layers of argillite, can hardly be explained in any other way than by supposing these lodes to have been formed by successive deposition at what was, at the time, the surface of the earth. There is, moreover, evidence that these laminæ were formed before the lodes were folded and contorted ; this is fur-

The crush or squeeze resulting from the folding of the cross anticlinals have occasionally produced apparent jogs in the leads which at the first glance suggest the passage of the lead from one side of a bed of slate or whin to the other, after cutting obliquely or at right angles across it, but without its continuity being broken. Two well marked instances of this form of disturbance came under my notice at Mount Uniacke. In one case, the lead after descending as a plain sheet of quartz several feet at an angle of 65° S., abruptly takes a horizontal course northward for the space of four feet, not, however, in a plane sheet of quartz, but in corrugations like barrel quartz, it then assumes a course parallel to its original direction, and as a plane sheet plunges downwards at the angle of 65° S.

In another instance the crush, instead of throwing the lead out of its course by a horizontal thrust, has acted in a direction from east to west, and the corrugations between the two planes in which the different parts of the lead are found, are vertical instead of horizontal, as in the first-named case. The first illustration may have taken place during the east and west folding, the latter during the north and south folding, for at Mount Uniacke as well as at Waverley there is very low, but distinctly marked cross anticlinal.

The effect of the movement is also seen in the remarkable bulging out of leads. Huge lenticular masses of quartz, probably of subsequent origin, are not unfrequently found asso-

---

nished by some remarkable specimens of the so-called barrel quartz which I took from a lode at Upper Stewiacke, and which consists of a bluish quartz in thin plates sometimes not more than one-twentieth of an inch in thickness, and presenting in some instances glazed surfaces coated with thin argillaceous films, and in others, pellicles of argillite having the thickness of paper. The surfaces of all these layers are deeply striated or furrowed at right angles to the axis of the larger convolutions of the bed, a result evidently due to a sliding of the layers of the quartz lode over one another during the corrugation of the strata which has here taken place near the summit the anticlinal. It seems not improbable that the corrugated structure of the lodes, which gives rise to the barrel quartz, is due to the difference in texture, and to the greater resistance to lateral pressure offered by the quartz layers than by the enclosing beds of clay and sandstone, which by their consolidation have given rise to the argillites and quartzites. There is, moreover, evidence that during the movement of the strata, openings and fissures were in some cases formed in these quartz lodes, giving rise to joints in which gold, metallic sulphurets, and carbonate of lime were afterwards deposited, apparently by solution and segregation from the adjacent parts of the lode."

ciated with a thin lead not more than a few inches in thickness. A mass 10 feet in diameter at the surface has been found to diminish at the depth of 18 feet to 2 inches.

Surface indications are not to be relied on as determining the number of leads in a given space. Like the thin beds of slate with which they are frequently associated, the auriferous quartz beds " give out" and " take up" again at intervals, not unfrequently constituting very thin and broad lenticular sheets; many leads, however, preserve tolerable uniformity for miles.

Hence it is impossible to speak with certainty of the number of leads in a given space, for surface indications do not always afford the requisite means for obtaining correct information.

In a shaft at Sherbrooke, at a depth of 90 feet, a tunnel was driven at right angles to the strike of the leads (across the metals) for a distance of 80 feet. Twenty-three leads were intersected, from 3″ to 12″ in thickness, whereas at the surface only ten had been discovered by costeening.

At Lawrencetown nine leads had been discovered within a space of 90 feet by costeening; a quarter of a mile to the east seventeen leads were exposed on the continuation of the same group, and within the same horizontal distance.

In a space of 120 feet at Waverley, twenty-seven leads, varying from one inch to twenty inches in thickness, were found by careful costeening. Broad bands of quartzite or Whin are frequently barren; and the association of leads with special rock species affords a convenient method of grouping them.

Where slates abound the leads are very numerous; and no true estimate of the auriferous value of a slaty series of beds can be formed except by tunnelling at right angles to the strike.

In Australia " the quartz veins occur throughout the lower palæozoic rocks, from the size of a thread to many feet in thickness. They have mostly a nearly true meridional direction, and are inclined either east or west, at angles varying from horizontal to vertical; occasionally they occur between the planes of the strata, more frequently those of cleavage, and they often intersect both. They are true mineral lodes, and perfectly analagous in their mode of occurrence to all other mineral veins, whether of silver, lead, tin, copper, or any other crystalline mineral." (1)

Veins frequently occur between planes of cleavage in the Nova Scotia districts; they are very numerous in one part of Mount Uniacke, and also in the country west of West Waverley. No instance of a cleavage vein having been worked in Nova Scotia is known to me.

In North Carolina the gold belongs to four different geological positions :—

1st. Drift gold.

2nd. " In stratified layers which are contemporaneous with the rock."

3rd. " In connection with seams and joints of the rock, and probably diffused in the mass."

4th. " In regular veins associated with quartz and the sulphurets of iron and copper."—(Emmons, Geology of North Carolina.)

Dr. Emmons lays stress upon the discovery first made by him in 1856, that the gold found in the bedded strata in North Carolina is of contemporaneous age with the rock. " If this view is correct gold is a sediment; and belongs, as I shall show, to the Palæozon period."

The rocks of North Carolina are of especial interest in connection with Nova Scotia geology, for it will be shewn in the sequel that the strata at Waverley are very probably of the same age as the gold bearing beds in North Carolina, and lie near the base of the Lower Silurian Series.

CROSS LEADS AND TRUE VEINS.

Every district has its cross leads. These occur in fissures produced by dislocation, or in some quartzites or Whin, possibly as shrinkage cracks. The first named may be very valuable, from their great depth, and possible accumulation of rich deposits of mineral in the fissures they fill. They are all segregated veins, no instance of an injected vein having been discovered in any district.

(1.) Selwyn—Geology of Victoria.

The true veins are not numerous, but sometimes they are exceedingly rich. None of the veins cutting the strata at Waverley have been worked. One side of the great dislocation at Montague is the seat of a true vein, loaded with arsenical pyrites; it is auriferous, but has not been worked. At Lawrencetown the vein filling a crack cutting the strata at a very small angle, presented promising appearances. At Mount Uniacke a small vein cutting the quartzite yielded several ounces to the ton. At Oldham true veins are numerous, and in some instances promising.

IX. — WAVERLEY LEADS.

Rejecting insignificant returns from trial assays of other leads than those enumerated below, the aggregate quantity of gold yielded by five leads at Waverley during the years 1862 to 1868, inclusive, has amounted to 45,000 ounces (estimated).

The worked leads are in ascending order,

1. Barrel Quartz Lead.
2. No. VI.
3. South Taylor or Union.
4. North Taylor.
5. Tudor.
6. Brodie or North Lead.

From these leads there has been extracted, according to official returns, the quantities of quartz and gold shown in the subjoined table during each year. The average yield being 10 dwts. nearly.

YEAR.	Quartz—Tons crushed.	Total yield in ounces.	Average yield per ton.			Average per man.
			oz.	dwts.	grs.	
1862	3,741	1,507	0	8	0	....
1863	6,754	2,380	0	7	1	$258 40
1864 (9 mo's).	6,979	4,491	0	12	17	297 80
1865	10,709	13,102	1	4	11	895 87
1866	17,286	10,486	0	12	1	584 31
1867	11,289	4,134	0	7	7	422 63
1868	8,401	3,242	0	7	22	....
Totals.....	65,159 tons.	39,342 oz.	10 dwt. nearly			

BARREL QUARTZ GROUP.

The Barrel Quartz Lead.

In the early history of Gold Mining in Nova Scotia, the Barrel Quartz was supposed to be a distinct mineral development, and as such the record of the yield of gold from this lead was distinguished from others. The following table shows the amount of quartz crushed and gold produced during the years 1862 and 1863 from the "Barrel Quartz:"

	Tons of Quartz Crushed.	Produce in oz.	Average.
1862	3592	1360	7½ dwts.
1863	2370	471	4 "
Total........	5952 tons.	1831 ozs.	5 dwts. 16 grs.

At Oldham there is a "Barrel Lead," which dips to the north at an angle of 60 degrees. It yielded in 1862 a minimum of 14 dwts. to the ton. The highest being 1 oz. 10 dwts. to the ton. The depth to which it was mined in that year reached eighty feet. In 1867 several corrugated leads were exposed at Oldham, and indeed in almost all the mining districts modifications of the Barrel Quartz of Waverley have been discovered, being doubtless in all cases originally horizontal beds of quartz, which have been subsequently corrugated during the process of the folding of the anticlinals or synclinals in which they are found. There is no reason to suppose that the peculiar corrugated or barrel formation has any influence upon the richness of the lead.

In East Waverley the Barrel Quartz Lead has a large accessible development. Its form there, to the depth of several hundred feet, is that of the rind of half a lemon, slightly compressed at its north side, flattened at the top, and cut clean and square off at one extremity, where it meets with the great upthrow running in part through Lakes William and Thomas.

There are several faults intersecting the barrel quartz on a course north 6 degrees east. Some members of this system of faults can be seen in the bare rock on areas 5, 4 and 3, they are from 4 feet to 40 feet between the walls.

The Barrel Quartz is cut clean off by a fault at the eastern extremity of the present workings. The displacement does not appear to exceed a few feet, but it would require special examination to determine the extent of the movement.

An excellent guide is afforded by the appearance of the Barrel Quartz, on the north-east corner of area 310, West Waverley. Here in the disturbed belt the lead is vertical, with a course S. 79 E., and the following section is visible :—

Whin.
Barrel Lead......................... 6 inches.
(Slate) Argillite .... 3 feet 0 "
Whin........ ....21 " 6 "
Lead .... 0 " 4 "
Slate........... .... 3 to 4 " 0 "
Whin.

In West Waverley the Barrel Quartz lead lies nearly hori-zontal, and but a few feet below the surface, (dependant upon the undulations,) forming the flat compressed crown of the an-ticlinal. It plunges rather suddenly to the south and north, as shewn on Section No. V. On area 189 the Barrel Quartz lead will dip gently to the west, and before it reaches the west main dislocation with gradually increasing dip, it will be about 1800 feet below the surface.

Below the Barrel Quartz there are four leads known to exist; that there are very many more accessible there can be little doubt. In subsequent pages a comparison is made between the Waverley anticlinal and the Mount Uniacke anticlinal, in which it is shown that great probability exists that below the barrel quartz a considerable number of gold bearing leads will be found.

THE ROSE GROUP.

No retures from this group. A few shallow shafts have been sunk on the Rose Lead.

THE TAYLOR GROUP.

The following leads have been worked in this group :—
1. No. VI. Lead.
2. South Taylor or Union.
3. North Taylor.

From the manner in which the accounts have been kept by the different companies working in these leads, it is impossible to obtain any correct information respecting the average yield of gold.

The following tables have been kindly furnished by W. H. Clarke, Esq.

Leads worked by Taylor, Waverley & Boston and Nova Scotia Gold Mining Companies, the number of shafts and depths, and the aggregate yield.

Name of Lead.	Shaft.	Depth.	Lead.	Shaft.	Depth.	Lead.	Shaft.	Depth.
		Feet.			Feet.			Feet.
N. Taylor.	1	135	S. Taylor	1	130	No. VI.	1	150
"	2	100	"	3	150	"	2	90
"	3	100	"	3	220	"	3	90
"	4	75	"	4	175	"	4	280
"	5	45				"	5	361
"	6	110				"	6	187
						"	7	120
						"	8	135

1. Aggregate yield, 7,903 ounces.
2. Dip of gold streak, East to West.
3. Shafts numbered from Muddy Pond east to Lake Thomas.

Leads worked by North American Gold Mining Company, the number and depth of shafts, and the aggregate yield.

	Shaft.	Depth.		Shaft.	Depth.
		Feet.			Feet.
North or Brodie vein..	1	60	Tudor vein..	1	120
" " " ..	2	120	" " ..	2	140
" " " ..	3	105			

1. Aggregate yield, 670 ounces.
2. Dip of gold streak on North vein, West to East.
3. No visible gold streak on Tudor vein.
4. Shafts numbered from East to West.

Leads worked by Rockland Gold Mining Company since May, 1863; number of shafts on each, and their respective present depths, with aggregate yield from same, including Barrel Quartz; also those worked by Lake Major Gold Mining Company since April, 1867.

NAME.	Shafts.	Depth.	NAME.	Shafts.	Depth.	NAME.	Shafts.	Depth.	Aggregate Yield.
Tudor Lead— Rockland Company	1	60 ft. Works Stp.	Brodie or North Lead	1	95 ft.	Union Lead, S. Taylor	1	120 ft.	
"	2	230 ft.	"	2	140 "	"	2	140 "	
"	3	190 "	"	3	160 "	"	3	170 "	
"	4	185 "	" Wrk'g Sa.	4	210 ft.	"	4	160 "	
"	5	180 "	"	5	175 "	"	5	145 "	
"	6	175 "	"	6	170 "	"	6	125 "	
"	7	173 "							
Lake Major Company	1	190 ft.	"	1	220 ft.				6884 oz.
"	2	195 "	"	2	225 "				
"	3	200 "	" Wrk'g S	3	230 "				
"	4	260 " Works Stp.	"	4	240 ft.				
"	5	380 ft.	"	5	220 "				
"	6	320 "	"	6	205 "				
"	7	310 "	"	7	195 "				
"	8	300 "	"	8	180 "				
"	9	295 "							3155 oz.

3

The following tables have been supplied by Mr. Burkner, showing the yield of gold from the Tudor Lead at different depths. It happens, unfortunately, that quartz from the North Lead was crushed simultaneously with quartz from the Tudor Lead, so that it is impossible to construct a diagram shewing the position of the rich auriferous zone of gold-bearing quartz with accuracy on either lead.

As a general fact it may be inferred that the zone of richest quartz lay between fifty-five and one hundred and ten feet from the surface. That on area 162 it descended to nearly 200 feet in depth, and that below 200 feet the average yield obtained in the crusher did not exceed 8 dwts. per ton. Mr. Burkner estimates that not less than from two to three thousand ounces were stolen by the miners.

It must not be supposed that eight pennyweights represented the average *total amount* of gold in a ton of quartz at a depth of 260 to 300 feet, that quantity having been obtained by the process employed at the mill, and it is safe to state, as shown subsequently, (Mining Economies at Waverley) that it does not represent the actual amount of gold which might have been obtained by at least 33 per cent. or one-third.

The average yield below 200 feet may be put down as below:—

Gold obtained by crushing.................8 dwts. per ton.
Escaped in the tailings (35 p. c.)............4   "   "
                                           ─────────
Total average yield per ton.............   12 dwts.

Monthly Returns of L. Burkner's Mill at Waverley, of Quartz from about 750 feet along the Tudor Lead for the year 1865.

		oz.	dwt.	oz.	dwt.
January.. 110 tons of western 300 feet....		153	3		
" 305 " of eastern 450 "		288	13		
Total for January				441	16
Febr'y ... 210 tons of western 450 feet...........				190	2
Western 300 ft. drowned this month.					
March ... 272 tons of western 300 feet....		605	6		
" 382 " of eastern 450 " ...		427	8		
Total for March..............				1032	14

		oz.	dwt.	oz.	dwt.
April....	205 tons of western 300 feet....	482	9		
"	298 " of eastern 450 "	320	1		
	Total for April.................			802	10
May.....	172 tons of western 300 feet....	384	10		
"	307 " of eastern 450 "	379	0		
	Total for May................			763	10
June	260 tons of western 300 feet....	645	17		
"	440 " of eastern 450 "	554	4		
	Total for June			1200	1
July.....	220 tons of western 300 feet....	445	0		
"	358 " of eastern 450 "	343	19		
	Total for July................			788	19
August..	300 tons of western 300 feet....	501	4		
"	476 " of eastern 450 "	473	15		
	Total for August			974	19
Sept'r....	237 tons of western 300 feet....	358	14		
"	358 " of eastern 450 "	363	19		
	Total for September			722	13
Oct'r.....	220 tons of western 300 feet....	366	11		
"	548 " of eastern 450 "	486	15		
	Total for October.............			853	6
Nov'r ...	270 tons of western 300 feet ...	201	3		
"	530 " of eastern 450 " ...	358	5		
	Total for November...........			559	8
Dec'r....	111 tons of western 150 feet....	99	11		
"	383 " of eastern 450 "	298	2		
	Total for December...........			397	13
6972 tons.				8727	11

		oz.	dwt.		oz.	dwt.	
2377 tons of western 300 ft.,		4243	8	Average,	1	14	per ton.
4595 " of eastern 450 "		4484	3	"	0	19	"
6972 tons.	750 "	8727	11	"	1	6	"

Besides this amount of gold, at least $50,000 to $60,000, or 2500 to 3000 ounces, if not more, were stolen by the miners during the same year.

The yield of gold during the last six months of 1864 was nearly the same as the average of 1865.

The yield during 1866 and 1867 gradually decreased (in the most western 150 feet of the lead rapidly,) until it did not cover the expenses.

The total working expenses (crushing included) have been up to 1866, about $10 to $12 per ton on the eastern part of the lead, and about $12 to $14 per ton on the western part. Since 1866 the lead has been worked $3 to $5 per ton cheaper.

Yield of the Twlor Lead in Areas 165, 164, 163, 162, 161 and 160 from the top to 110, 145, 230 and 330 feet in depth, respectively.

Depth.	Areas 165, 164 and 163.	Area 162.	Area 161 and east. ⅓ part of 160.	Area 160.
First 5 feet, whole depth 5 feet	0 oz. 10 dwt.	0 oz. 15 dwt.	0 oz. 13 dwt.	0 oz. 5 dwt,
Next 10 ft. (to 15 ft.) " 15 "	0 oz. 5 to 7 dwt.	0 oz. 10 dwt. to 12.	0 oz. 7 dwt. to 10.	0 oz. 3 dwt,
Next 15 ft. " 30 "	0 oz. 10dw. to 12¼w.	0 oz. to 15 dwt.	0 oz. 13 dwt.	0 oz. 3 dwt.
Next 25 ft. " 55 "	1oz. 2dwt. to 15dwt.	1 oz. to 1 oz. 5 dwt.	1 oz. 0 dwt.	0 oz. 3 dwt.
Next 35 ft. " 90 "	1 oz. 5 dwt.	3 oz. to 3 oz. 10 dwt.	2 oz. to 2 oz., 10dwt.	0 oz. 5 dwt.
Next 20 ft. " 110 "	1 oz. 0 dwt.	1½ oz. to 2 oz,	- 1 oz. to 1¼ oz.	0 oz. 3 dwt.
Next 15 " " 125 "	0 oz. 12 dwt. to 14.	1 oz. 0 dwt.	0 oz. 10 dwt,	Work stopped.
Next 20 ft. " 145 "	0 oz. 10 dwt.	0 oz. 17 dwt. }	0 oz. 3 dwt,	
Next 50 " " 195 "	0 oz. 10 dwt.	0 oz. 15 dwt. } *	Work stopped.	
Next 25 " " 220 "	0 oz. 8 dwt.	0 oz. 8dwt., eastern ⅔ of area.		
Next 10 " 230 "	0 oz. 8 dwt.	0 oz. 8 dwt.; most E. ⅓ pt.; W. only 3dwt.		
" 100 ft. " 330 "	0 oz. 7 dwt.	Work stopped.		

* Western part of area poorer already, probably down to 6 dwts, and at last to 3 dwt.

Western 300 feet gave 1 oz. 14 dwt, per ton.   Eastern 450 feet gave 0 oz. 19 dwt. per ton.

X.—THE " GOLD STREAK."

In every district in Nova Scotia it is remarked that the gold frequently "runs in streaks;" that is to say a zone of rich auriferous quartz occupies a certain breadth in the lead, while to the east and west of that zone the quartz is comparatively poor in the precious metal. It is also found that in different districts the "Gold Streak" has a different angle with the horizon, and that sometimes the course of the rich zone is coincident with the ripples or swells in the leads,— also that the Gold Streak varies in direction in different leads.

At Montague the Gold Streak dips at an angle of 45 degrees to the west, so also do the corrugations in the lead.

At Sherbrooke in some mines the Gold Streak on the south side of the anticlinal dips to the east at a high angle, and on the north side to the west at about the same angle.

At Lawrencetown the dip is westerly at a low angle. The dip of the corrugations in the same.

It is probable that in each lead the Gold Streak has a course peculiar to itself, with an easterly and westerly trend. Known facts respecting the Gold Streak are too few and too indefinite to permit of any conclusion being drawn for any number of leads, but where one lead is taken into consideration, much useful information may be obtained by studying the structure of the lead and the direction of the " Streak."

In the shallow synclinal at Lawrencetown for instance, the dip of the Gold Streak being westerly at a low angle on the south side of the synclinal, its dip will probably be easterly at the same angle on the north side. On an anticlinal if the streak or zone dip easterly on the south side, it will be found dipping westerly on the north side, in the continuation of the same lead or sheet of auriferous quartz. At Montague there are two very rich zones on the same lead about 520 feet apart, dipping west at an angle of 45 degrees. The breadth of one zone is about 300 feet, of the other 250 feet; the yield of gold in each has been tolerably uniform, and averaged 3½ ounces to the ton. On the west side of these zones the yield diminishes abruptly to 5 dwts. per ton ; on the other side it shades off to 3 dwts. per ton.

The distribution of the zones at Sherbrooke leads to the inference that the gold was originally deposited in belts from the oceanic waters, whether influenced by accumulations of organic matter or otherwise. It would be a simple matter to explain the structure of the Gold Streak, on the supposition that organic matter determined the deposition of the metal in belts or zones, for it is easy to conceive accumulations of stranded organisms on subaqueous beaches in a shallow sea in the form of long narrow bands. Organic matter determines the deposition of most metals from solutions, and whatever intermediate combinations and decompositions took place, accumulations of organic matter may have been the proximate cause which determined the distribution of the gold in zones or belts. According to this view the direction of Gold Streak will probably differ slightly in each lead, but there will be a general parallelism in a considerable number of adjacent leads, and the direction of one zone will be a clue to several.

But other and more important deductions may be drawn when attention is given to one particular lead. The course of the Gold Streak being once known, it can be traced through all the deviations produced by anticlinals, synclinals, dislocations, and in general almost all varieties of disturbance.

From Mr. Burkner's table on page 36 it appears that the average yield of the Tudor Lead, between the depths of 55 feet and 100 feet from the surface, was as follows, from east to west :—
Breadth of Zone, 55 feet.

Mean yield on areas 165, 164, 163.....	450 feet.	22 dwts.
" " area 162	150 do.	36 "
161) And one-third of 160 }	200 do.	24 "
Mean yield of two thirds of area 160...	100 do.	3⅔ "

The falling off in the west 100 feet of area, 160 is not only sudden but extreme. But it must be remembered that on this area the work was stopped at a depth of 110 feet. It is worth while to consider what probabilities exist of discovering the rich zone at a greater depth.

An inspection of the section showing the form of the east and west anticlinal, points out the remarkable coincidence that in area 160 (or more properly area 201, where Mr. Burkner's shafts are really situated, as shown on the large plan in the Mines' Department), the strata dip suddenly to the west at an angle of about 50 degrees. At Mr. Burkner's last shaft they dip N. 50 W., and are already to the west of the crown of the arch, produced by the lateral crush or squeeze between the walls of the great dislocations.

Hence the zone of rich auriferous quartz, dipping with the strata, has already begun to plunge to the west at an angle of about forty or fifty degrees, and must be sought for below the depth of 110 feet, at which depth the work was stopped.

The course of the rich zone west of area 201 will be nearly parallel to the axis of the anticlinal, through areas 202, 203, south part of 157, 156, 155, &c., but descending westerly at an angle of about 45 °, in a word being roughly parallel to the intersection of the Tudor vein as shown in the east and west section.

Mr. Clarke states that no visible Gold Streak was met with in that part of the Tudor Lead which passes through some of the properties east of Mr. Burkner's areas. But the " Streak" on the North Lead dipped from west to east, and the " Streak" on the North Taylor, South Taylor and No. 6 Leads, dipped from east to west. It is much to be regretted that no reliable data exists from which diagrams showing the auriferous zones on these leads can be constructed. The circumstance of the quartz from all being mixed before crushing makes it impossible to collate the necessary observations. The general fact is stated as the result of observations during the time the work was going on.

XI.—GOLD AT DIFFERENT DEPTHS.

The evidence now supplied by the California mines, which are generally situated on leads similar to those of Nova Scotia,[1] that is to say on beds of quartz, but of Jurrassic age instead of Silurian age, tends to disprove the supposition that the quantity of gold per ton diminishes as the depth increases. Some of the deepest mines in Grass Valley do not become

---

(1.) Hunt, page 11, Gold Regions of Nova Scotia.

sensibly impoverished in depth, "as, in common with all the mines of that district, they are at the present time quite as productive as they have ever been at any period since the commencement of operations."[2]

Among the instances cited by Phillips, in 1866, are the—

1. North Star, worked on its inclination to a depth of 700 feet.
2. Eureka Mine, sunk to the 400 foot level.
3. Hayward's Mine (Amador County) worked on its inclination to a depth of 1250 feet, and increasing in richness.
4. Allison Branch, 500 feet.

Dr. Hunt quotes Mr. Michel's opinion on this important point. Mr. Michel says:—

" If the results obtained during the last few years in Nova Scotia show that the veins are irregular in richness, they demonstrate their continued richness in depth. I saw specimens rich in visible gold, extracted from depths of 105, 156, 180 and 215 feet respectively, in the districts of Mount Uniacke, Renfrew, Wine Harbour, and Sherbrooke, and I am aware that a shaft on the Tudor vein at Waverley yields at the depth of 185 feet quartz affording more than an ounce of gold to the ton. Such veins as these just mentioned, which, with a great regularity of form and position, have presented alternations of poor and rich quartz to the depths already cited, will probably be found to offer similar variations to much greater depths. To abandon a working on account of a momentary impoverishment of the lode, as has too often been done in this region, is therefore unwise ; and in a large enterprise, where mining is carried on in several veins at a time, the richness of some of these may always be counted upon to compensate for the temporary poverty of others. I am of opinion that an unnecessary discouragement has had as much to do with the failure of certain gold-mining enterprises in Nova Scotia as the want of scientific knowledge and the neglect of proper preparations, and that many of those now abandoned as unprofitable, *will be again taken* up with advantage."—*Gold Regions of Nova Scotia.*

At Waverley, Mr. Clarke found rich quartz at the depth of 361 feet in No. VI. Lead, and the work was stopped on account of the expense of hoisting the water with horse whims.

The origin and structure of the auriferous leads is wholly opposed to the supposition that any diminution in richness is

(2.) Phillips.—The Mining and Metallurgy of Gold and Silver.

likely to take place. If the leads are, as already stated, inter-stratified auriferous beds of quartz, of contemporaneous age with the Slates, Whin and Quartzites, and deposited like these from oceanic waters holding gold in solution, together with most of the other metals, it follows necessarily that unless a subsequent movement of the gold took place, which is not generally probable, except where segregated veins occur, there can be no valid reason for the assumption that the richness of the leads diminishes with the depth. On the contrary, the probability exists that the sheets of quartz constituting the leads, will be auriferous all the way from one district to another, although they may not be accessible. The Tudor lead, as well as all the other Waverley leads, are indefinitely prolonged in all directions like the interstratified slates and Whin. They may " thin out," as before stated, but they " will take up again." Beneath the railway, west of Waverley, the Tudor Group no doubt exists at a depth between two and three thousand feet, and if it were possible to reach the leads there, they would be found to be auriferous. The gold deposits of Nova Scotia are only limited by the area of the Province, but they are accessible only when the auriferous rocks are exposed on the eroded summits of anticlinals or the eroded edges of synclinals.[1]

XII.—COMPARISON BETWEEN THE GEOLOGICAL STRUCTURE OF WAVERLEY AND MOUNT UNIACKE.

A section in detail across three thousand feet of the strata at Mount Uniacke, made last summer, enables me to institute a comparison with the Waverley beds, and to draw some general conclusions which show a remarkable similarity between the structure of these districts.

(1.) The following are some of the anticlinals and synclinals where the auriferous rocks come to the surface.

ANTICLINALS:

1. Lawrencetown (Double or Twin Anticlinal.)
2. Waverley. 3. Renfrew. 4. Oldham.
. Mount Uniacke. 6. Sherbrooke. 7. Wine Harbour, &c.

SYNCLINALS:

1. Lawrencetown between the Twin-anticlinals. 2. Montague. 3. Isaac's Harbour, (west side, Lone Star Mine.)

The east and west anticlinal at Mount Uniacke is similar in form to that of Waverley, and may be described as a sharp fold with an overturn dip on the south side. The summit has not been flattened or compressed, and it is probable that the overturn is greater than at the last named district,—and bends over to the south instead of to the north.

The rocks are generally similar in composition, and are arranged in alternating beds of Whin and slate, with a bed of gritty quartzite not less than 380 feet thick where the section was made, and without visible partings of slate. Succeeding this enormous band of quartzite are alternating beds of Whin and slate, the first named greatly preponderating.

The strata at Mount Uniacke, from the axis of the anticlinal, in which direction the section was made southwards, may be represented as given below.

The cross anticlinal appears to be very gentle, so that the outcrop of the band of quartzite, and consequently of most of the leads, if no great dislocations have taken place, will be that of a very long and narrow ellipse, much flattened on the south side and bulging out on the north side.

SECTION AT MOUNT UNIACKE.

	Feet.	Rocks.
Axis of anticlinal to arsenical group of leads......	475	Alternating beds of Whin and slate with leads.
Arsenical group to centre of Twisted Slates.	200	Alternating beds of Whin and slate with leads.— Twisted slates about 50 feet thick, and micaceous.
Centre of Twisted Slates to base of Great Quartzite Band.	110	Whin and slate.
GREAT QUARTZITE BAND...	380	Very coarse at base, in fact a grit, with grains generally as large as a mustard seed, then gradually becoming finer as it approaches the summit, where it is a very fine light-coloured rock.

Dark coloured slates with plumbaginous surfaces, interstratified with bands of " Whin.".	20	Leads.
Whin with thin bands of slate—in the centre the slates are twisted......	775	Leads.
Dark coloured slates with plumbaginous surfaces, with thin bands of Whin.	60	Leads.
Heavy bedded " Whin " with a few thin bands of slate	750	Leads.

Total thickness measured.. 2770 feet.

A coarse grit or quartzite, much resembling the coarse grit at Mount Uniacke, has been already described as occurring at Waverley, where it is especially distinguished by concretionary forms, and fossils supposed to be the Palæotrochis of Emmons. Hence it has been marked on the map as Concretionary Quartzite.

In the following section made by Mr. Clarke in the spring of last year, the concretionary quartzite occurs in that part of the section enclosed within brackets, and it is the 431 feet of strata at Waverley composed of 421 feet of " Whin," and 9 feet 3 inches of slate, which I propose provisionally to place as the equivalent of the 380 feet belt at Mount Uniacke.

Mr. Clarke's Section on Areas 370, 315, 304, 249, 238 *and* 183, *on North and South Course.*

NORTH.

	Feet.	Inches.	
Whin............	51		....
	1	0	.... Lead.
Slate..	6	5	....
	1	4	.... Lead.
Slate	5	6	....
	1	0	.... Lead.
Whin............	30	6	....
Slate	26		....

	Feet.	Inches.	
*Whin	178		⎫
Slate	1	3	
		6	Lead. ⎬ Probable equivalent of the great band of Quartzite at Mount Uniacke.
Whin	161		
Slate	8		
Whin	83		⎭
	0	3	Lead.
Slate	1	3	
Whin	15	6	
Slate	2	2	
Whin	36		
Slate	35		
Whin	80	6	
		1	Lead.
Whin	5		
		2	Lead.
Whin	5	3	
		10	Lead.
Whin	77		
		2	Lead.
Slate	1	3	
Whin	64		
		3	Lead.
Whin	99		
	45		Concealed.
Whin	34		
Slate	41		

Probable equivalent on the north side of the anticlinal (area 185 W. W.), consisting of 110 feet of strata north of Graham's Lead, of 132 feet of the Whin Band 178 feet thick in Clarke's Section, on areas 238 and 249 W. W., and marked with an * in the section above.

NORTH.

	Feet.	Inches.	
Whin	8	8	
		4	Lead.
Whin	5	9	
Slate		8	
		1	Lead.
Whin	7		
		1	Lead with Slate.
Slate	2	9	
Whin	5		
		1	Lead.

	Feet.	Inches.	
Whin	25		
		2	...............Lead.
Whin	5	3	....
		1	...............Lead.
Whin	6	9	....
Slate...............	1		....
Whin	11	3	....
		7	...............Lead.
Whin	6	3	....
		4	...............Lead.
Whin	22	6	....
Total Whin........	103	5	
" Slate	4	5	
" Quartz and Slate	2	15	
Total Rock........	110	1	

The difference between 110 feet 1 inch and 137 being due to difference in dip.

The season of the year has prevented any search being made for fossils or concretions at Mount Uniacke resembling those in the concretionary quartzite at Waverley, for it was not until after the snow had fallen in November last that the identity was suspected.

The "dark colored slate with plumbaginous surfaces," occurring above the quartzite at Mount Uniacke, agrees in position with the plumbaginous slates of the Taylor group at Waverley.

Should the identity between these strata in the two districts be established, the following conclusions will be reasonable :—

1st. That a large number of gold-bearing quartz leads lie underneath the lowest lead known at Waverley.

2nd. That on the assumption that no very considerable differences in the aggregate thickness exist between the strata at Mount Uniacke and Waverley, there is a belt of auriferous strata about six hundred feet thick concealed beneath the Barrel Quartz at Waverley which is exposed at Mount Uniacke.

3rd. That the Taylor Group may be identified at Mount Uniacke associated with the " dark colored slates with plumbaginous surfaces."

4th. That the equivalent of the rich Tudor group may be found at Mount Uniacke.

5th. That the majority of worked mines are on leads which will be found below the barrel quartz at Waverley.

There is no reason to suppose that the great quartzite belt at Mount Uniacke is destitute of leads or slate partings in other parts of the district. It has been already observed, that both slate and leads not unfrequently " thin out " and " take up " again ; that they often form thin lenticular sheets, where Whin occurs in massive beds. When leads are found in slate they are generally persistent.

It is this intermittent form of some leads which has led to the opinion that they are segregated veins filling longitudinal cracks produced by the folding of the strata. It must be borne in mind that independently of the slaty structure of many leads as described by Dr. Hunt, the pressure to which the strata were subjected during the folding, could not have been less than that of a mass of nine thousand feet in thickness, and, possibly, an incumbent ocean superadded. Under such pressure the formation of fissures would be problematical.

XIII.—COMPARISON BETWEEN WAVERLEY AND LAWRENCE-TOWN.

The structure of Lawrencetown is that of an east and west anticlinal, with a fold or synclinal near its summit, or it may be better described, perhaps, as two east and west anticlinals, separated by a shallow synclinal.

It has been before stated that a curly plumbaginous slate is characteristic of the Taylor Group at Waverley. In the shallow synclinal at Lawrencetown this curly plumbaginous slate has been recognized, and traced from the synclinal southwards until it plunges down the south side of the south anticlinal.

Assuming that this is the equivalent of the curly slate at Waverley, the following conclusions are admissable :—

1st. That the leads worked at Waverley in the Werner Group and the Bennet Group are the prolongation of the Taylor Group of Waverley.

2nd. That the Belt and Vance Groups at Lawrencetown are identical with the Tudor and South Groups at Waverley.

3rd. That the Shanghaie Group at Lawrencetown is the equivalent of the Rose Group at Waverley, with part of the Taylor Group.

4th. That the Barrel quartz group of Waverley and the leads worked at Mount Uniacke (McKintosh. West Lake, Queen, &c.,) will be found in a synclinal form north of the Shanghaie Group at Lawrencetown ; but south of the Werner Group they will be several hundred feet below the surface.

I do not wish it to be understood that I present these comparisons as *establishing* an identity, but rather, as not improbable deductions from observed facts, which if borne out by future investigation, cannot fail to exercise a very important influence upon gold mining throughout the country.

Should future observations show them to be true, in careful and scrupulous hands, they will be found excellent guides, not only in prospecting but in mining, and they will go far to set the question at rest respecting the origin, structure and permanency of the leads, and supply a clue to] discover the law which has determined the direction and distribution of the " Gold Streak " or rich zone of auriferous quartz in different districts.

XIV.—MINING ECONOMICS AT WAVERLEY.

MILL WORK.

In all gold mining countries experience has established the rule, that in general it is more profitable to crush large quantities of quartz of low standard, than small quantities of rich mineral on a limited scale.

In seven important gold producing counties in California the cost of extracting quartz from the mines (1861) [1] varied from one dollar fifty cents per ton to thirteen dollars per ton.

(1.) Ashburne's Tables.

In one mine the cost was .... $13 00   per ton.
In one   "   "   "   .... 8 00   "
In three "   "   "   .... 6 00   "
In four   "   "   "   .... 5 87 to $5   "
In one   "   "   "   .... 4 50   "
In two   "   "   "   .... 3 73 to $3   "
In seven "   "   "   .... 2 93 to $2   "
In two   "   "   "   .... 1 50   "

In 13 of these mines the average yield per ton is under $15.

In Australia "when, as at first, the cost of crushing and amalgamating a ton of quartz amounted to some 80s. ($20), a very small proportion of the auriferous veins of the colony could be treated with advantage; but now that the total expense of raising and treating a ton of rock by steam-power has, under favourable circumstances, been reduced to about 16s. 4d. ($4.08). there are numerous reefs throughout the gold-mining region affording satisfactory results, and many others that would do the same if extensively and judiciously worked." [2]

In 1866 the returns from the various districts in Victoria, shewed the following results :—

Mining District.	Tons Crushed.	Total Produce.		Yield per Ton.	
		oz.	dwt.	oz.	dwt.
Ballarat	238,503	58,157	3	4	21
Beechworth	130,519	118,495	19	18	3.7
Sandhurst	244,807	118,743	10	9	16.8
Maryborough	79,552	44,967	14	11	7.3
Castlemaine	124,734	85,667	3	13	18.5
Ararat	43,711	33,868	18	15	11.9
Totals	861,468	459,895	7	10	16.2

Hence it appears that the average yield of gold per ton in Victoria was 10 dwts. 16.2 grains in 1866.

In Nova Scotia the average yield per ton during the same year was 15. dwts 14 grains, or nearly one-third more than in Victoria.

(2.) Philips : The Mining and Metallurgy of Gold and Silver.

The present cost of mining in Nova Scotia is no guide to what might be the cost of extracting mineral from the lead and gold from the mineral if judicious management were general.

At Mr. Burkner's mill (water power) the amalgamation takes place in the battery; there is no concentrating apparatus, and the tailings flow into the stream and are lost. Küstel, in his "Processes of Silver and Gold Extraction," states that "if the proper proportion of quicksilver, and regular times of charging be observed, when the ore contains heavy gold (800 fine), *sixty* to *seventy-five per cent.* may be saved in the battery and the copper-plated platform; but light gold, (300 to 400 fine) like Washoe gold, gives a less favorable result. A great many fine particles of amalgam adhere together, involving also manganese scum, if present, and form spongy, blackish lumps, which are so light as to float, and on account of being coated with foreign matters, will not unite with the accumulated amalgam. Of this amalgam but very little can be saved; it floats over blankets, copper-plates, or ripples."

At the Port Philip Mining Company, in Australia, where the tailings are regularly assayed, they are found to yield on an average 2 dwts. of gold per ton, the average quantity obtained from the stampers not exceeding 7 dwts. per ton in 1865 and 6 months of 1866.

It is safe to assume that where arsenical iron ore is so abundant in the quartz as at Waverley, not more than 66 per cent. of the gold is saved even by the most careful amalgamation. In other words, 33 per cent., or one-third, escapes and is lost in one of these forms:

1. It forms a spongy amalgam, and floats away.

2. It escapes amalgamation, being coated with a compound of arsenic.

3. It escapes in arsenides and sulphides of iron.

4. It escapes amalgamation, being coated with grease derived from the candles of the miners.

Forms No. 2, 3 and 4 can be saved by a buddle or rocker, or by blankets; and a portion of No. 1 also, arrested.

At the Port Philip Works the pyrites is dressed up by concentration to an average of three or four ounces of gold to the ton of material. "This is then sent to the roasting furnace, and afterwards ground in Chilian mills with mercury, and an average of about 85 per cent. of the assay contents of

4

the gold is thus extracted. The cost of operating on the pyrites, including the buddle, roasting, grinding, loss of mercury, etc., averages about $5 per ounce of gold obtained."

In 1865 Mr. Burkner crushed 6,972 tons of quartz, which yielded 8727 ounces of gold, averaging 1 oz. 6 dwts. 12 grs. per ton. It is a fair estimate to suppose that 30 per cent. escaped in the tailings, or more than $58,000 worth of gold ; Of this enormous loss, fully two-thirds, or $38,000, might have been saved by adopting the process common in all well-regulated gold-mining establishments in California or Australia, whether in the form of buddles, blankets, or any other suitable device.

The following diagram from "Phillips' Mining and Metallurgy of Gold and Silver," shows the series of operations rock undergoes in some of the best mills in the neighborhood of Grass Valley, California, where amalgamation in the Battery is discarded. Ninety per cent of the gold in the mineral are obtained by this process.

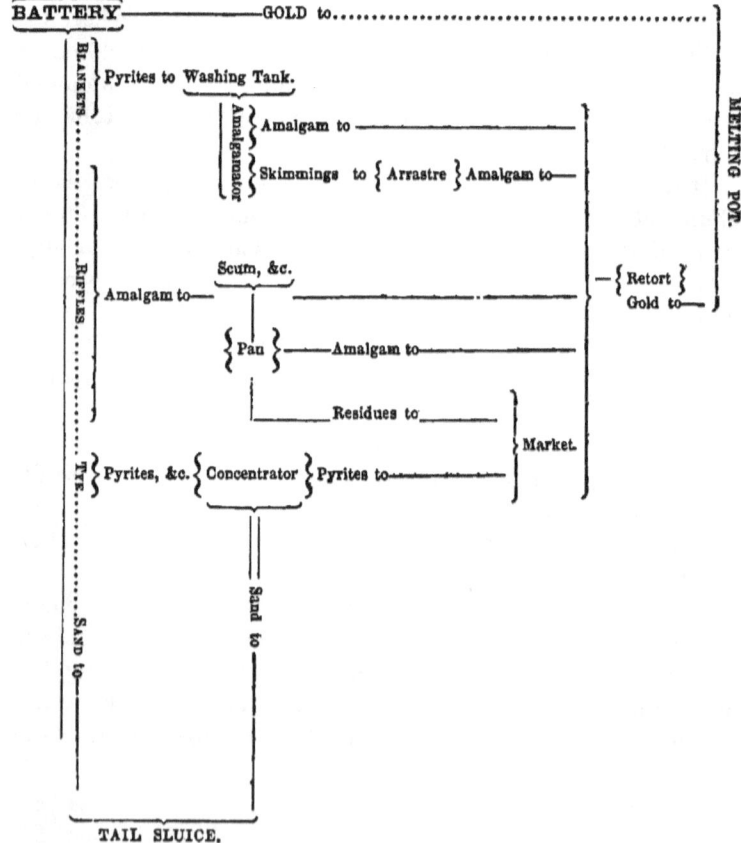

A correspondent of the "Mining Gazette" (April, 1868) says :—

"Some three or four years since, two tons of thoroughly concentrated material collected at Waverley, were sent to the Swansea works (Wales), and yielded a nett return of $1050; this gave renewed energy to the first parties, and induced others to try it, and further lots were sent—some to Swansea, and some to Freiburg, but neither were sufficiently remunerative to make it much of an object. Analytical assays showed it to contain only about $115 per ton, while the practical yield was very considerably less, and the nett returns less still. But it should be explained that the first lot was the concentrated result of former concentrations, and comprehending a large quantity of quartz; while the other lots were merely a collection of the heavier particles which had passed through the mill and then indifferently (though at considerable expense) washed over again by hand, and in this consistency shipped. The rationale being—increase of quantity at expense of quality. But it may be important to state, the original ores which produced all these results were comparatively free of sulphurets."

In the following pages an attempt is made to show how the adoption of proper processes might have considerably diminished the cost of extracting the gold, and make the present average yield per ton not only pay all expenses, but yield a handsome profit. In criticising past operations in gold mining in Waverley it must be borne in mind that the industry is still new to the country; that much energy and enterprise has been exhibited, but generally by those without experience in mining economies or knowledge of the elementary principles of structural geology. The impression, too, is very prevalent, there as elsewhere, that without any previous training or study, two or three years experience in one gold mine is sufficient to fit a man to fill any situation in any gold mining district. Preconceived ideas derived from desultory or ill-directed reading often produce very prejudicial effects. It is common to find practical miners entertain the idea that all quartz is of igneous origin, and that all the leads in Nova Scotia are injected veins. Starting from such a basis, it is no wonder that men are led into extravagant and hopeless expenses in search " for veins," and cherish delusions for which there is not a shadow of foundation. Take for instance the following para-.

graphs from the " Mining Gazette," of Feb'y., 1868, under the
heading " Gold Mining Review ":—

" Perhaps there is no district in the Province promises so
permanent and extensive operations as Lawrencetown.   The
lodes present this interesting feature, viz: they depart from
the vertical at different angles, and by measurement it is supposed that the whole 28 veins *will unite* into one main vein at
a point between 200 and 300 feet from the surface.   What the
probable effect of this union will be, the experienced miner
alone can judge."

The leads referred to, which are symmetrically bedded like
the " coats of an onion," in a synclinal or valley fold, were
thought by the writer of the paragraph quoted, to be injected
veins, and as a natural consequence of their supposed conver-
gence, to proceed from one main vein " coming from below."

As an illustration of the necessity of attention to structural
geology, the following case which occurred at Waverley may
be cited.   In attempting to discover the south outcrop of the
Tudor Lead, measurements were correctly made to the axis of
the anticlinal, (the general structure of the rocks and leads
being recognized and understood,) and the expectation was
entertained that the southern outcrop would be struck at the
same distance south of the axis as the northern outcrop was
north of it.   This would have been the case if the anticlinal
were symmetrical ; but it has an overturn dip to the north ;
and the dips on the north side are greater than those on the
south, hence the southern outcrop of the Tudor lead is many
yards further from the axis than the northern outcrop.   The
time and money spent on the search were consequently lost,
but the same energy and spirit which directed this exploration
beneath the deep boulder drift of West Waverley would no
doubt have been successful if the unsymmetrical arrangement of the sides of the anticlinal had been known.

The amount of money and time spent in prospecting in Nova
Scotia is very large, and sometimes the search is made with
astonishing perseverance, guided by the auriferous boulders
on the surface.   In explorations of this kind, there is no
general guide, perseverance in searching for the lead according to the lay of the land being generally attended with success, but in endeavours to trace a lead in a district covered

with drift, intersected by faults, and disturbed by cross anticlinals, a knowledge of the elements of structural geology is
essential. Just as in mining economies, the skill which makes
a difference of one pennyweight per ton, frequently determines the fate of a valuable mining property. In the case of
the fine water power mill at Waverley, seven pennyweights to
the ton is stated not to pay expenses; eight pennyweights
would leave a small profit, and nine pennyweights, it is said,
would secure a profit of forty dollars a day. Operations are
now suspended, because the quartz is said to yield only 7
dwts. per ton according to the present system of working.
Subsequently it will be shown that there is every probability that the quartz now contains upwards of 10 dwts. to
the ton, although it yields only 7 dwts., and that by system
and machinery and consequent reduction of expenses, it might
be made to give an equivalent to 10 dwts. to the ton. The
same observation applies in other forms to all the other properties in the district.

Mr. Burkner's mining expenses up to the close of 1866
averaged $12 a ton. Since that period they have averaged $4
a ton less, or $8 a ton. This latter statement is corroborated
by the Chief Commissioner of Mines, who states in his report
for 1867 that "there is no place in the Province, so far as I
can learn, where mining is so economically carried on, and
crushing so cheaply done, as in this district. A lead is now
worked averaging 15 inches in thickness, at a depth of 300
feet, at a cost of 8 dwts. to the ton."

From Mr. Burkner's tables we learn that at a depth of 330
feet on the Tudor Lead, the yield was 7 dwts. per ton, and the
mineral not paying expenses the work was stopped.

It has been shown that it is probable that one-third of the
gold was lost in the tailings, which were allowed to escape
from the copper plates in front of the Battery directly into the
River. This would give a total average of gold in the quartz
of 10 dwts. 12 gr., of which 7 dwts. was saved, and 3 dwts. 12
grains lost. Assuming that 75 per cent. of the gold in the
tailings could be recovered by the usual processes, at a cost of
one-fourth, this would leave a profit on the tailings of 1 dwt.
16½ grains, and swell the total yield to 9 dwts. 15 grains per
ton. A round buddle, with a bed 18 feet in diameter, and

whose axis revolves at the rate of 3 or 4 revolutions per minute, will work up from 35 to 40 tons of tailings in 24 hours. A Rotating Buddle will do the same amount of work in much less time, and may consequently be made of smaller diameter.

By the substitution of proper machinery much manual labor in milling could be saved. Ten men were employed during twenty-four hours in breaking and feeding thirty-five tons of quartz; why should not this work be done by four men feeding a " Breaker " with Hopper, and moved by the surplus water power? Each of the stone-breaking machines at the Port Philip Company's mines break 8 tons of quartz per hour at a cost, including wear and tear, of about 10d. per ton. One of these machines would break 35 tons of quartz in 4 hours and a half at a cost of about $5 by water power, the estimate 10d. (stg.) a ton being based on steam power. Hence with a " Breaker " and " Hopper," instead of manual labor, a saving of at least $3 a day might be effected, and the risk of gold being stolen during this part of the treatment reduced to a minimum, by which it is not improbable a still greater saving might be effected.

I have selected as an illustration of mining economies at Waverley the method of treating the quartz at the cheapest mill, namely, one driven by ample water power. All the other mills in operation are driven by steam power, amalgamation takes place in the Battery and on tables, but no effort is made to concentrate the tailings. As long as quartz continues to yield the unusual average of 1 oz. to 1 oz. and 10 dwt. to the ton, the economical treatment of the tailings is not a matter of vital importance, but when the average diminishes to 9, 8 and even 7 dwts. per ton, it becomes one on which, other things being equal, the continuance of active operations depends, provided that those operations are necessarily limited to one or two leads.

XV.—SYSTEM OF MINING.

The following analysis of mining operations at Waverley are suggestive both with reference to the causes which have led to the present depression and to the future of the district when systematically worked.

North Lead (Brodie Lead.)

Length of outcrop in West Waverley.....7800 feet.
Length worked ....1800 "
Number of shafts........................ 23
Greatest depth of shaft................. 240 feet.
Average distance of shafts apart.......... 78 "
Mean depth of shafts.................... 185 "
Ratio of worked to unworked portion of lead
    to the depth of 240 feet.............One-fourth.

Tudor Lead.

Length of outcrop in West Waverley..... 7400 feet.
Length worked. ....2200 "
Number of shafts...................... 31
Average distance of shafts apart.......... 70 feet.
Greatest depth of shafts............... . 380 "
Mean depth of shafts........ .... 218 "
Ratio of worked to unworked portion of lead
    to the depth of 218 feet............Five-seventeenths.

North Taylor Lead.

Length of outcrop in West Waverley.....7200 feet.
Length worked....................... 800 "
Number of shafts...................... 6
Greatest depth of shaft................. 135 feet.
Average distance of shafts apart.......... 133 "
Mean depth of shafts.................... 94 "
Ratio of worked to unworked portion of lead
    to the depth of 94 feet ....One-ninth.

South Taylor or Union Lead.

Length of outcrop of South Taylor Lead in
    West Waverley...................7000 feet.
Length worked ....1200 "
Number of shafts................ 10
Average distance of shafts apart.......... 120 feet.
Greatest depth of shafts............... 220 "
Mean depth of shafts.................... 153 "
Ratio of worked to unworked portion of lead
    to the depth of 153 feet............One-sixth.

Number VI. Lead.

Length of outcrop of Number VI. Lead in
    West Waverley............................6600 feet.
Length worked................................ 600 "
Number of shafts............................ 8
Average distance of shafts apart......... 75 feet.
Greatest depth of shafts................. 361 "
Mean depth of shafts..................... 176 "
Ratio of worked to unworked portion of lead
    to the depth of 176 feet ....One-eleventh.

The ratio which the quantity worked of the five leads bears to the quantity unworked, to a mean depth of 165 feet in West Waverley, is as 181 to 1000, or about one to six.

In round numbers, one-sixth part only of the five leads enumerated above has been worked to a mean depth of 165 feet; and assuming that they are capable of being worked to the depth of 800 feet, the proportion of these leads still remaining untouched in West Waverley, would be nearly thirty times as great as the part which has been taken away. But besides these five leads, there are about forty other leads, many of which have not been even tested. A comparison of the foregoing tables, with the large plan, will be sufficient to show that mining at Waverley has been pursued without system.

The North Lead and the Tudor Lead are, on an average, sixty feet apart at their outcrops, their dips being nearly the same. The number of shafts sunk by different companies on these leads, within a mean distance of 2000 feet, is fifty-four, having a mean depth of 200 feet. This is equivalent to a shaft to every superficial area of *forty-seven feet square.*

On area 155, for example, there are four shafts on the Tudor Lead and three shafts on the North Lead—the breadth of the area being 150 feet. On area 102 there are three shafts on the Tudor and three on the North Lead, the same on areas 164 and 102. On the property of one company there are 8 shafts on the North Lead in the space of 450 feet, and 9 shafts on the Tudor Lead within the same distance. The leads being but sixty feet apart. Two main shafts, with suitable hoisting and pumping machinery, and cross galleries, would have been ample, and the saving in labour and time would have greatly reduced the cost of mining the quartz.

Mr. Burkner states that "up to 1866 the total working expenses on the Tudor and North Leads amounted to $10 to $12 per ton on the eastern part of the lead, and from $12 to $14 per ton on the western part. Since 1866 the lead has been worked $3 to $5 per ton cheaper." How is this to be explained? especially as the cost increases with the depth. The average yield per ton in 1865 was 24 dwts., 11 grains. In 1866 it fell to 12 dwts. 1 grain, or about one-half; hence, probably, economy in working became a necessity. But this absence of system or economy ought not to detract from the value of the lead.

A remarkable instance of want of foresight in a most important department of mining economics is presented in the construction of one of the largest steam crushing mills. The site selected for this mill is so low that the tailings, as they leave the mill, are now required to be hoisted by a revolving wheel, furnished with buckets, to a sluice, where they have an opportunity of escaping over the accumulated heaps near the mill, but without any attempt at concentration, or saving any of the gold which they undoubtedly contain. This is equivalent to employing power, machinery and labour, to get rid of 1 dwt., 16½ grains of gold per ton. A buddle to concentrate the tailings and save the gold, could have been constructed at far less cost than the present ingenious contrivance to hoist the tailings out of the way.

XVI.—GENERAL OBSERVATIONS.

The practice of mixing quartz from different leads and crushing the whole together is to be condemned. It is impossible by the adoption of this method to ascertain whether a lead is paying or not. A poor lead worked at the same cost as a rich lead may neutralize all the benefits which would be obtained if the rich lead were worked alone. Each lead ought to be crushed by itself, and a statement of the result with the cost of mining the quartz recorded. This can be done without any difficulty in mills with from ten to twenty stamps without retarding work if system is adopted. Plans of all the workings are also essential, showing at least monthly progress. In case a fault is discovered in one lead, and difficulties should arise in ascertaining the effect of the disturbance, it can be speedily reached in a neighboring lead, and the question whether it is an upthrow or downthrow, or throw to the north or south, or two or more of these movements combined, settled generally without difficulty; but if no monthly plan of workings is kept on record, all is confusion. With the single exception of a plan and section made some years ago by Mr. Bell of the works on a few areas, together with a lithographed plan of the whole district showing the position of the several properties, I was unable to obtain any plan of surface workings, much less any plan of underground workings, and the agents of the different companies uniformly informed me that none to their knowledge were in existence.

The absorption of all returns to pay large dividends is as a rule as fatal an error in gold mining as in most other enterprises. When the different mines were yielding very handsome returns, it was most unwise to suppose that such unlooked-for prosperity would continue for any length of time. Nevertheless it appears that nearly all profits were at once divided amongst the shareholders, and no reserve fund permitted to accumulate. Hence when the returns grew less the necessary means to provide machinery for deeper workings were not forthcoming, and, as a consequence, most of the establishments were closed.

The narrowness of the properties is a great objection to permanent operations. Several companies at Waverley have only 450 feet on the leads. If, owing to the absence of appropriate pumping and hoisting machinery, the works are stopped at a depth of 300 feet, it is very easy to calculate the duration of a company with such a small quantity of available lead. The absence of any regulations defining the space which different companies shall leave between the workings on the same or adjacent lead is likely to become a fruitful source of trouble. In one instance at Waverley the agents of two companies decided not to touch the quartz within four feet of their boundary on either side, with a view to prevent by means of an eight foot dividing wall the water from one mine draining into the other. This agreement, I was informed, was faithfully kept on one side and as grossly abused on the other, the whole of the four feet of quartz being removed. The consequence is that the works on one mine being stopped, the proprietors of the other have been vainly endeavoring to drain both on account of leakage through the dividing wall, which unfortunately has hitherto defied all their attempts to arrest.

It is an error to suppose that because a lead diminishes in average so as to be worked at a loss, that it will necessarily continue poor. All experience in gold mining tends to prove that all leads or veins are more or less intermittent in yield. If we may be guided by Montague, the nearest district to Waverley, and a synclinal fold of the same auriferous belt, the rich auriferous zones follow one another within a few hundred feet. It has already been stated that many of the leads in California have a bedded structure, and they are profitably worked at a depth of 800 feet with intermittent degrees of richness. At the same time proper machinery for hoisting and drainage must be adopted in order to arrive at this result, which, it need scarcely be observed, cannot be obtained if shareholders insist on a division of all profits, without leaving any reserve for contingencies, and subsequently refuse to raise additional funds when the period for their application arrives.

It is to be feared that this system is too commonly pursued in Nova Scotia, and there is reason for supposing that other districts will soon be in the same condition as Waverley. But there is no present cause for apprehension that with systematic mining, conducted on proper business principles, the leads will be less profitably worked in the future, or that there is any danger whatever of the yield of gold diminishing under the judicious management of mining properties. On the other hand, the remarkable uniformity and continuity of the leads, their great number in a small vertical space, their bedded structure, which implies indefinite prolongation, and the high per centage of gold they contain, are convincing proofs that when capital, skill, and forethought are combined, a very large proportion of both West and East Waverley will yet be profitably mined for many years to come.

As a rule, abundance of quartz of low standard, say from eight to ten penny-weighths to the ton, with water power to

work the crusher and buddles, is preferable to small rich
leads, yielding from one ounce to two ounces to the ton. Experience shows that these rich leads are liable to become reduced to the general standard.

Leads in slate are most to be relied on, and it frequently
happens that the slate is sufficiently auriferous to be worked
at a profit. At Sherbrooke, Wine Harbor, and Montague, the
slate forming the wall rock of the leads, (and in cases where
the lead is a mixture of slate and quartz,) is crushed to a large
extent and found profitable. This is a consideration of mo-
ment in estimating the probable value of leads where cheap
crushing is applicable.

The influence of Nova Scotia winters on mining operations
is sensibly felt in weak establishments, or where an ill-regulated
supply of water is alone available for milling purposes. In
well-organized mines the effect of frost in retarding operations
is not appreciably felt, and for certain kinds of work it is be-
neficial, as it arrests the supply of surface water. The following tables show the returns during each quarter of the
year for five years :—

	1864. Ounces.	1865. Ounces.	1866. Ounces.	1867. Ounces.	1868. Ounces.
Quarter ending March 31	4,010	5,101	5,018	5,410	5,457
" " June 30.	5,158	7,837	3,915	7,502	4,954
" " Sept. 30.	5,393	5,467	7,184	7,583	5,047
" " Dec. 31.	5,456	6,044	7,086	6,818	5,064
Totals.........	20,017	25,449	23,203	27,313	20,522

The total annual yield as given above appears different from
the published official tables of returns, but this apparent difference arises from the official return being made up from 30th
September of one year to 30th September of the year next
succeeding. In the above table, in order to institute a proper
comparison, showing the influence of the winter season, each
year is taken separately and entire.

XVII.—AGE OF THE GOLD-BEARING ROCKS OF NOVA SCOTIA.

Allusion has been made to the fossiliferous and concretionary quartzite or grit of Waverley and Mount Uniacke. The coarse portions of these deposits consist chiefly of rounded grains of quartz about the size of a grain of mustard seed cemented together. The Waverley rock is more ferruginous and darker colored than that of Mount Uniacke. Both contain grains of a lavender colored and semi-translucent quartz.

The Waverley beds contain a large number of fossils which resemble the *Palæotrochis minor* and *Palæotrochis major* of Emmons, besides numerous concretionary forms. The presence of these fossils, if they are identical with those in the North Carolina beds, probably establishes the age of the gold mining rocks of Nova Scotia, and shows them to lie near the base of the Lower Silurian system, and to belong to the upper part of the Potsdam formation and lower part of the Calciferous formation, and to underlie the great mass of Serpentines and Red Slates discovered by Dr. Honeyman in Antigonish, which belong to the Quebec Group.

Dr. Emmons enumerates the following succession of rocks in North Carolina, in which gold not only occurs in bedded deposits of quartz, but is also in the strata with which the quartz beds are interstratified.

In ascending order:—

1. Talcose Slates passing into Silicious Slates. Thickness undetermined.
2. Brecciated conglomerates. 300–400 feet.
3. Slaty Breccia associated with horn-stone.
4. Granular Quartz, sometimes vitrious and filled with fossils and silicious concretions of the size of almonds. 200–300 feet thick.
5. Slaty Quartzite, with a few fossils, about 50 feet.
6. Slate without fossils, 40 feet.
7. White Quartz, more or less vitrified, filled with fossils and concretions. 700 to 800 feet thick.
8. Jointed Granular Quartz, with only a few fossils.
9. Vitrified Quartz, without fossils. 30 feet thick.
10. Granular Quartz, no fossils, thickness very great, but not determined.

Dr. Emmons considers that one of the most interesting facts connected with the *Palæotrochis* is that the rock in which it occurs in North Carolina is itself auriferous. " Gold has been obtained in large amounts from the fossiliferous beds themselves, over one hundred thousand dollars having been obtained by washing the debris of this rock."

Some of these beds, Dr. Emmons states, consist almost entirely of fossils, and intermixed with silicious concretions which are almond shaped and frequently contain the fossils. Age Lower Taconic of Emmons, or Lower Calciferous and Upper Potsdam. At Waverley the concretionary forms vary from half an inch to 4 inches in diameter. They are generally oval in shape, but sometimes round, with a depression in the centre. Attached to some of them are numerous arms, all symmetrically arranged. These structures are exceedingly difficult to remove, the grit in which they are found being very hard, with irregular fracture. In East Waverley the forms are very numerous. In West Waverley the cast is far more frequently seen.

www.ingramcontent.com/pod-product-compliance
Lightning Source LLC
Chambersburg PA
CBHW021228260626
47172CB00002B/651